SEALed

Outcome

Marissa Dobson

Published by Dobson Ink
Printed in the United States of America
ISBN-13: 978-1-946474-23-0

Acknowledgement

I would like to take a moment to thank everyone who helped me make *SEALed Outcome* happen.

SEALed Outcome was originally titled, *SEALed in Texas* and was part of Cat Johnson's Hot SEALs Kindle Worlds. First, I would like to thank Cat Johnson, for asking me to be part of her Kindle Worlds. It was truly an honor to work with you and all the other authors on board. Second, if you haven't checked Cat's books out yet, please be sure you do. You won't regret it.

I decided to do some rewrites before republishing *SEALed Outcome*. As much as I enjoyed being part of Cat's world, I've decided to remove the Hot SEALs world. During the transition, I've changed SEALed Outcome to stand alone.

With every book, there's a whole team who work together to produce the final piece. Without my critique partner, as well as my editing and proofing team, the book wouldn't shine as it does. Thank you, Felicia Sullivan, for working this book into your schedule even with my tight deadline. Thank you, Brynna Curry for editing this book and your amazing turn around.

Last but certainly not least, I would like to thank my amazing husband, Thomas. Those of you who read the dedications and acknowledgements in my books will see that he's mentioned in each of them. That's because he is my biggest supporter. I don't know if I would have ever published my first book without him. He's incredible and I couldn't have asked for a better soul mate. I love you, Thomas.

Chapter One

Rescue

Trever Alexander didn't even work for Safety First Security—not yet anyway—yet there he stood in the sweltering Texas heat on assignment. He was supposed to be considering their job offer, not getting firsthand experience on what the job would entail. Instead, Lucas, the founder of Safety First Security, and Trever's friend, Ethan, came to him with a situation which required someone with his unique skill set.

"Over and over in the field you somehow managed to get out of impossible situations. She needs that now. If there's anyone that can get her out of Texas, it's you. Your brother's plane…it's her only chance."

Ethan pushed and said the right things to make him uneasy, and in the end, even though it felt like a setup, Trever now stood in Texas. Maybe it wasn't a setup but a test instead. There was something that made him edgy about the way they brought him into this assignment. There were more than enough members of Safety First Security to handle the situation. They didn't need him, especially before he had committed to their team. So why pick him for this task?

He dug his cell phone out of his pocket and leaned against the side of his rental truck. It was time to find out more about this woman he was supposed to rescue. Information had been scarce when he left, and that hadn't sat well with him. Why send him across the country if they didn't know who she was? He hit Ethan's name and brought the phone to his ear.

"You there, Trever?" Ethan's voice came through the phone's speaker.

"I'm standing outside in the parking lot across from where you told me to be." He scanned the motel looking for anything that might give him a clue as to who he was looking for. The migraine he was trying to fight off was only escalating from the horrible heat and the blazing sun overhead. "You going to tell me what the fuck I'm doing in Hell?"

"Hell…" Ethan let out a sharp laugh. "Texas heat is nothing like the sandbox."

A flash of memories from his days in the sandbox flickered behind his eyelids until he ran his fingers over his eyes, pinching the bridge of his nose. "What the hell am I doing here? I left this state in my rear view a long time ago." His voice was deep as he fought to remain focused instead of being dragged into the past.

"During the last contact we had with her, she mentioned she was staying at that motel, room twenty-three. Find her and get her out of Texas."

"Who is she?" He was quickly growing tired of having to pull information from Ethan, and if this was how Safety First Security worked, he wasn't sure he wanted to be involved. He didn't like going into a situation without all the facts.

"Check your phone. Her information and picture are waiting for you." With that, the line went dead.

"What the hell, Ethan!" There was something going on. This mission was too secretive. What was Ethan hiding? He pulled his phone away from his ear and pulled up his email. A few clicks later and he was staring at the reason Ethan had only dribbled out a little information at a time.

A picture of Allyson Mason filled his phone screen and his chest tightened. Her beautiful green eyes stared up at him, but the sparkle they once held was gone, leaving behind a hollowness. The smile stretched across her face appeared to be forced, and her shoulders were squared as if she was expecting something to happen. He knew she had once been determined to be an elementary school teacher and now she was on the run. What had happened?

He forced himself to scroll down past the picture to the text: *She got tangled up with a local gangster after a drug deal went bad. The authorities are closing in on him, but until they get their case tied up, she needs to leave Texas. I'd do this, but she needs you more than her cousin.*

"Fuck!" He locked the screen and shoved the phone back into his pocket.

Ethan had known all along who the woman in danger was, but he hadn't told him. Would he have come to Texas if he had known Allyson was in danger? He wanted to say no, that the road leading to her was closed, but damn it if he wouldn't have dashed off to rescue her even if she hated him for it. A drug deal? Had she gotten into *drugs*? What happened to the sweet innocent girl he left behind?

Needing answers, he hopped back into the truck and drove across the street. If there was someone looking for her he needed the getaway vehicle close. In case they needed to get out of there quickly, he reversed the truck into a parking spot next to the steps that would lead up to room twenty-three. He wasn't sure if she had been mindful enough not to stay on the first floor or if it was just a stroke of luck. Either way, he was grateful she had that extra protection while she waited for him. Being on the second floor would allow her to scan the parking lot from an advantage point and might give her a few minutes to get away if anyone showed up looking for her.

Before he climbed out of the truck he considered for a moment throwing on his jacket to conceal the gun strapped to his hip, but in the end he decided a jacket in this weather would draw more attention than the gun itself. He was in Texas and half of the residents carried, so he'd blend in fine. Plus, there wasn't a chance he was leaving his gun behind in the truck. He stepped out and with a quick look, he headed for the stairs. If she was waiting in her room, they could be out of there and back to his plane before anyone was the wiser.

He doubted this was going to be that easy though.

When no one answered the door, he picked the lock and stepped into the hotel room. Quickly shutting the door behind him, he took in the room before him. Even in the faint light peeking around the bathroom door, he could tell the whole room needed a deep cleaning. It wasn't a place he expected Allison to ever willingly stay. Hell, he'd rather be back in the sandbox than stay in that room for the night.

The only sound was the shower running. Alone and scared, yet she was taking a shower with only the standard lock on the door. She hadn't even bothered to throw the latch. It wouldn't have stopped anyone but the sound of the bolts being tugged from the door would have been enough noise to be heard over the shower.

The water shut off, leaving behind only her faint humming. Not wanting to scare her, Trever stepped into the shadows next to the bathroom door and waited. Running through different scenarios he considered his next move. What would be the least frightening and the quietest way to make his present known? A moment later she stepped out of the bathroom, a thin towel wrapped around her body. Needing to make sure she didn't scream like a banshee at the sight of someone in her room, he stepped up behind her and clapped his hand over her mouth.

Chapter Two

Terror

Fear raced through Allyson, turning her stomach and icing her blood. She couldn't move, couldn't fight back. Her worst nightmares were alive and well in the dirty motel room in Texas. Showering had been a terrible idea but after days on the run she needed to clean up. At the time she thought it was worth the risk. Now, she knew it wasn't. It had been the final blow, allowing them to capture her.

This is the end; I'm going to die.

Tears burned behind her eyelids. She knew Trever would be disappointed if he could see her now. Though he had taught her self-defense tactics, in the moment she needed them she couldn't remember an ounce of what he taught her. She stood there frozen, clutching the towel to her body.

Again, I failed you Trever.

"Allie, don't scream."

Allie? No one calls me that, no one but…no it can't be…

Hearing her nickname rocked her world, but not more than what she saw when her captor tipped her head to the side allowing her to see him.

Trever!

He kept his hand pressed to her mouth, holding it together and keeping her quiet. She had to be seeing things. She wanted so badly for him to be there to help her get out of the mess in which she found herself that she was hallucinating.

"Stay quiet. I'm going to remove my hand." His voice was barely above a whisper, yet she recognized it without a doubt.

His hand slid away from her mouth, but he kept his hand on her shoulder, keeping her close. Even after his hand was gone, she couldn't speak. The words died on her tongue. It took her a moment to pull herself together and form not only words but complete sentences.

"What are you doing here?" Her gaze stayed glued to him. "What the hell were you thinking putting your hand over my mouth and scaring the shit out of me?"

"I didn't want you to scream." He stared at her as if it was obvious why he did it. "It seemed like the best idea at the time. Otherwise a woman screaming might have brought attention that we don't want."

"Doubt that." She shook her head, not wanting to think about all that went on in a cheap roadside motel like this. "How the hell did you get in here?"

"I knocked and no one answered. So, I picked the lock."

"You picked the lock." She stumbled back and sank down onto the hard motel bed, the weight of the whole situation weighing heavily on her shoulders. "What are you doing here? Shouldn't you be in Iraq or somewhere, defending our country?" The minute the harsh words were out of her mouth she wanted to take back the roughness of her tone. She wanted to rush into his arms and have him hold her and tell her that this was going to be okay.

The sudden shift as he turned away from her was as clear as if he had thrown a wall up between them. He didn't want to talk about it and it only made her eye him more closely. The bathroom light was the only light in the room, casting a yellowish tint over everything. She could see the jagged scar across his cheekbone, and more marring his toned arms. Had something happened? Had he been injured?

"Trever?" she prompted.

"The only thing that matters is I'm here and I'm going to get you out of Texas. Now get dressed, we should be leaving." He moved to the other side of the room, his back to her, so she could change in privacy.

For a brief moment she had forgotten she only had a thin towel rapped around her body, leaving her practically naked. Without taking her eyes off his back she tugged the duffle bag that was on the edge of the bed closer. She unzipped her duffle bag and grabbed a tank top and jeans from within. She got dressed quickly and ran her fingers through her wet hair. Water droplets dripped onto her back, and the top of her tank top, but at least she was clean.

"You can turn around." Standing next to the bed she looked over at him. "I can't leave Texas."

"The fuck you can't." He now stood near the window, his attention split between glancing at her and looking out the window. "You're in danger here."

"Don't you think I realize that?" Her voice rose, which was better than giving in to the tears she wanted to shed. How had everything worked out like this? It was supposed to be a simple run to the store, then Anthony threw everything away and dragged her down with him.

"No, I don't." Trever turned back to look at her, his hand gesturing toward the door. "Otherwise you'd have been more careful. What the hell were you thinking, not even bothering to put the latch on the door? Are you hoping they catch you?"

"I...I...didn't think..." she stammered, knowing she had messed up. If Trever had gotten in without her hearing a sound, *anyone* could have. Someone else could have been waiting for her when she exited the shower completely unaware.

"You're right, you didn't think, and you could have gotten yourself killed."

He stood there unmoving as if she went through this type of shit all the time. She was out of her element and she knew it. It was why she'd called Ethan.

"You're the fucking SEAL, not me," she spat. "It's not like I run for my life every other day. I don't know what the hell I'm doing!" She sank down onto the bed again and stared at the floor. "Maybe I shouldn't have run. If I'd stayed I—"

"You'd be dead," He finished for her. He stepped away from the window and came around the bed to stand in front of her. "A drug deal? Damn it, Allie, are you hooked on that shit?"

"What?" She looked at him, blinking as she tried to adjust to the sudden swing in the conversation.

"If you're messed up on that shit I need to know. I can't have you strung out. In order to get you out of here I need you with a clear head."

"I thought you knew me better than that, Trever. I don't do drugs." Tired of her emotions pulling her in two different directions she forced herself to look away from him and let her gaze fall onto the duffel bag that held everything she now owned, which wasn't much. "Just get out. I don't need your help."

"I think you do."

"You left me." The words were out before she could stop them. That simple statement was the root of the newest turmoil inside her and was the one reason she was rejecting his help, though she hadn't meant to verbalize it. She didn't want him to know she still missed him.

"That's not what this is about."

"Everything changed when you left." She pulled her bag close and zippered it. "Please just go. I can't do this. I can't stand by and see you walk out of my life again."

"Let me get you out of here, and if you still want nothing to do with me, fine. But until someone else can protect you, you're stuck with me." He squatted down in front of her. "Allie, I'm not going to leave you here unprotected, so you might as well stop. No matter what you think, you're important to me."

"I called Ethan..." She'd have a few choice words for her cousin if she saw him again. He knew what had happened between her and Trever and still he sent him. It was like her cousin had no respect for her emotions.

"I know, and he asked me to come find you. I'm going to take you back to Montana. You can stay with him until—"

"Until what? Until they find me and kill me? Until I off myself because I can't live with this constant fear? Let's be realistic here for a moment, Trever. They're not going to stop until I'm dead. There's no convincing them I had nothing to do with any of it. That I happened to be in the wrong place at the wrong time. Trust me, I've already tried."

"*What?*" He leaned back, nearly knocking himself off balance and falling on his ass before he adjusted to remain on the balls of his feet. "What do you mean you've tried? Are you crazy? You shouldn't have been anywhere near them. They're dangerous."

"Really?" She stared at him with wide eyes, sarcasm dripping from her statement. "I'd have never guessed. How do you suppose I got these?" She held up her wrists to him, showing him the raw rope burned skin from where she had been tied up.

"What happened to you? Ethan said you were fine." He took her hand into his and looked down at the wounds. "Are you hurt anywhere else?"

"I'm fine." She tried to pull her hand out of his but he held on tight enough that she couldn't without fighting him. "What was I supposed to tell Ethan?"

"The truth. That's always a good place to start."

"Kind of like us? Forget I said that, this isn't about us or the past." Her chest ached from being torn between her wants and fears. "He was across the

13

country and no matter how injured I was he couldn't have gotten here any faster. Not that he came anyway."

"He sent me." He brushed his thumb over her knuckles. "How'd you get away?"

"I—"

He shot up, dropping her hand and reaching for his gun. "Get in the bathroom. In the tub, stay there, nice and low until I call you." His voice left no room for questions. "Go."

Trusting him completely, she did what he asked. She stepped into the bathroom and shut the door just as the main door came crashing in. Her heart beat frantically against her chest as she climbed into the tub. Bangs and gunshots echoed within the room and she crouched lower.

Even with the knowledge they had found her, and she'd end up dead, all she could think about was Trever's safety. He meant so much to her and he was in this because of her. *Please let him be okay.*

Chapter Three

Escaping

The minutes stretched on until Allyson thought she'd scream if she had to spend another minute crouched in the tub waiting for them to bust down the door and drag her out of there. She knew they'd kill her, but after the stunt she'd pulled they wouldn't make it quick. They'd want her to suffer. She glanced around the bathroom, looking for anything she could use as a weapon. A towel wasn't going to do. Maybe the back of the toilet? If she could get it off without making any noise, she could throw it at someone or hit them over the head. It might give her enough time to get away.

What am I thinking? I'm not just going to run if Trever's out there hurt.

She scooted closer to the toilet and wrapped her hands around the top piece of porcelain. The quietness had her easing it off gently, trying to avoid scraping against the back of the toilet.

What if he's dead?

She strained to hear something, anything, even the sound of someone breathing, but she couldn't hear anything over her own heartbeat.

Keep it together.

The door handle turned and she grabbed ahold of the porcelain, bringing it back toward her body in one quick movement. She didn't care about the noise as the two pieces clinked together. She wasn't going back, even if the alternative was death. Holding tight to the porcelain lid she rose, ready to attack as the door flung open revealing a bloody Trever.

"Let's go. Now!"

"You're alive." The porcelain slipped from her grasp, falling to the floor with a bang and shattering. Slivers of porcelain flew through the air, littering the floor, but she didn't care about anything other than him.

"It takes more than a few bullets to kill me." He glanced down at the now shattered remains. "Though having that bashed over my head might have changed things."

She climbed out of the tub and went to him, wrapping her arms around him. "I thought…"

He hissed and straightened as if she'd hurt him, then his arm went around her waist. "Shh, Allie." He squeezed her a little tighter before pulling back enough to look down at her. "I'm fine, but we've got to go. By now, someone would have called the police and they'll be on their way. We can't be caught here." He kept his arm loosely around her waist and guided them out of the bathroom.

She stumbled over the remains of the only chair the room had offered and her gaze took in the blood and…

"Oh heavens…"

Two dead bodies now lay sprawled out on the motel room floor, blood seeping into the thin carpet. Judging by the knife wounds and broken bones, the man closest to her appeared to have put up a good fight, before his neck had been snapped. While the other one closer to the door had been shot, blood and brain matter seeped out of where his skull used to be.

"Don't look, Allie." Without letting her go, Trever snatched her bag off the bed and led her toward the door.

"You killed them."

"It was either them or us. Which would you have preferred?" He glanced out into the hallway, checking both ways before pulling her out with him. "My truck is at the bottom of the steps. No matter what happens get to it and go." He shoved the keys into her hand.

His words stopped her in her tracks for a moment before he pulled her along, leaving her no choice but to walk or be dragged.

"I'm not leaving you," she stated.

"They're not after me, they're after you, so you'll do what you're told." On the way down the stairs he used his body to block hers as he checked to make sure no one was waiting for them there. "The GPS is already programed. Follow it and I'll meet you there."

"I can't do this without you." Even as the words left her mouth, she knew they sounded more like a whine than she'd intended. He was in this because of her and she wasn't going to leave him behind.

"Damn it, Allie, I don't know if there are more."

"Then we'll find out together." Sirens blared in the distance, drawing closer. "We've got to do it quickly or it won't matter."

He let go of her and put both hands on his gun. They made it down to the first floor without encountering anyone and he nodded toward the black pickup. "Get in."

She watched him holster his weapon then did as he asked, checking the parking lot as she opened the passenger door. No one was around. The other travelers staying at the motel must have been frightened away from gathering areas and were now hiding in their rooms. The fewer people that saw them the better their chances were of getting out of Texas without further incident. What happened afterwards though? It wasn't like the drug dealers wouldn't cross state lines to track her down. She was the only eyewitness of a murder that could put them behind bars. They weren't going to let her live to tell her tale.

Trever pulled open the driver's door and climbed in, holding his side.

"Let's get out of here."

She took her bag from him and handed him the keys. "You're injured."

"I'm fine." He started the truck, threw the gearshift in drive, and gunned it out of the parking lot just as the cops were coming down the road toward the motel. They were a couple of streets back, too close of a call, especially if they would have encountered anyone else on their way to the truck.

"No, you're not." She scooted across the seat and gently lifted his hand from his side. "The blood's yours, isn't it?"

He clenched his jaw and focused on driving. "I said I'm fine."

Allyson forced herself to take a deep breath. The rage that was bubbling within her wasn't for him. None of this was his fault, yet she almost lashed out at him. He was an easy target at the moment, but he didn't deserve her anger. He rode to her rescue when she needed it and risked his life to protect her.

"Please, let me look at it, Trever."

"Allie, it's not the first time I've been shot. I'll be fine."

"Shot?" Her mouth went dry at the thought and her chest tightened. He might have broken her heart when he left her but she still loved him. The thought of him almost getting killed because of her was like a knife in the back. He took a hard left, pushing her into his side, and forcing him to suck in air between his teeth.

"I'm sorry…this is all my fault."

"Tell me what happened, Allie."

"Huh?" She was taken off guard by his statement and for a moment forgot why her hand was on his thigh.

"You said you don't do drugs, so explain to me how a bad drug deal got you into this mess."

"I'll tell you *if* you let me look at your chest." Fisting a handful of his shirt, she gently tugged it out of his jeans.

"Under different circumstances I'd think you just wanted me naked." He took the hand closest to her off the wheel. "I told you I'm fine, the bullet went straight through."

"I want to see for myself." Carefully she peeled the blood-soaked shirt up and he gingerly adjusted in his seat so she could slide the shirt off his arm revealing the wound on his side where a bullet had grazed him. Even though it was a couple of inches long it wasn't too bad and the bleeding was minimal. His shoulder was a different story. The sight of blood seeping from the hole just below his collarbone was enough to make her lightheaded. "Damn it, Trever, you've been shot twice."

Chapter Four

Wounded

From the pain screaming through Trever's body he was surprised it was only twice. Every muscle in his chest hurt, but there wasn't time to deal with it. It wasn't a mortal wound, he'd survive as long as he stopped the bleeding, and it wasn't his first time being shot. The handgun hadn't done a tenth of the damage he'd suffered overseas. He had to stay focused and get Allyson out of the area. There was an hour drive between them and his plane. Even longer before he got her to safety.

"We've got to take you to the hospital."

"No." He merged the truck onto the highway and put his foot down harder on the gas.

"You need stitches."

"They'll ask too many questions we can't answer. Hospitals are required to report gunshot wounds to law enforcement. It won't take them long to figure out where we were when I was shot. So, no hospitals, I'll deal with it in a bit."

Just a little further and he could attend to it before the blood loss rendered him unconscious. He needed to put a little more distance between them and the city.

"You're bleeding."

"I *know*." He gripped the steering wheel and swerved into the next lane to pass the slow moving car in front of him. "Reach into the bag in the back seat. There's a first aid kit somewhere in there. Just tape some gauze over it so I don't bleed all over the truck. Otherwise the rental car company will get suspicious."

"You'll bleed through it." She leaned over the seat and dug into the bag. "We need to stop. Maybe we can pack the wound or something. I don't know—"

"Allie." He brushed his hand on her thigh and the pain as he moved his shoulder rocked through him. "I'm going to be fine, I promise."

"Forgive me if I don't believe you, but I remember the last promise you made to me and you broke it." She grabbed the kit and turned back to him. "Let's just stop somewhere."

"Soon." The pain in her voice sent another stab of agony through his chest, only this time it wasn't from his wounds, but from the hurt he'd caused her. The memory of what she was talking about flashed in his mind.

They sat on the tailgate of his old beat-up truck, overlooking her family's ranch. The horses chewed on hay in their enclosure, while off in the distance the cows mooed. There was something peaceful to it all, like that was where they belonged, and he was giving it all up. Well not everything, he still had plans, only they'd changed from taking over his father's cattle ranch to joining the Navy. He still planned on marrying Allie and making her the mother of his children. Boot camp, and then he'd propose. He needed to know he could do this before he could ask her to spend the rest of her life with him. If he failed, he didn't deserve her.

"Joining the Navy will change nothing. Boot camp will fly by and we can be together. I promise." He pulled her closer and when she turned her head toward him their lips met.

"Ssss…*shit*." The memory faded away when she pressed a piece of gauze to his shoulder, stealing his breath from his lungs. Stars danced before his eyes and darkness threatened to close in on him before he blinked it away.

"Sorry. Pressure will help stop the bleeding. Lean up so I can get another

22

piece on the back."

"Just put tape over it. You don't need to hold it there." He forced himself to lean forward, giving her enough room to deal with the exit wound. The warm blood dripping down his back made him all too aware that it was bleeding heavier than the entrance wound. It would be bigger and ragged from the force of the bullet tearing out of him.

"You drive and let me deal with this." She pressed the pad against his back and held it in place. "Lean back against my hand."

"Woman, you're becoming awfully demanding." Doing what she asked, he took the highway exit, leading them onto a quieter road.

"Where are we going?" Pressing her hands to each side of his shoulder she glanced out the window.

"One of the SEALs from my old team, Mac Garcia, has a cottage up this way. Actually, it's his wife's cottage. It used to be her grandmother's. We'll stop by there so I can clean up. I can't head to the airstrip with blood all over me. It's a private airstrip, but still, it would raise too many questions."

"You're going to break into your friend's place? Don't you think we've committed enough felonies for one day?"

"It's not breaking and entering if you know where the spare key is. Trust me, Mac isn't going to mind." He pulled the truck to the side of the road and adjusted enough to pull his cell phone from the confines of his pocket. "Would it make you feel better if I called him?"

"I just meant…oh forget it." Frustrated, Allyson let out a sigh and pressed against his shoulder.

"It's safe, I swear. Mac's a good guy. We've gone through Hell together and I've trusted him with my life. He's not going to care if we stop by his place." The cell phone in his hand vibrated and he glanced down at the screen—Ethan. "Your cousin is calling to check on my progress." He hit talk and then the speakerphone button. "I've got her. Say hi, Allie."

"Bastard." Allie spat.

"Nice to hear your voice too, Allyson." Ethan chuckled before clearing his throat and getting down to business. "Well, Trever, I hear you got into some trouble back at the motel. Left behind a few bodies."

"I did what I had to do and if need be I'll face the consequences." He didn't want to have this conversation with Ethan, at least not with Allie in earshot. He had killed before but he wasn't a stone cold killer. With every drop of blood on his hands, he suffered mentally for it. However, he had never killed someone who hadn't deserved it. This time there hadn't been another choice, at least not one that would have left Allie alive. "After I get Allie out of Texas I'll deal with it."

"I don't think there will be any reason for that. It appears they had a shootout between each other, resulting in their deaths. I guess it was over some promotion they were up for."

"Huh?" Trever's eyebrows knitted in confusion at Ethan's statement.

"You heard me. That's the official police statement. Guess the big man has someone on the force that's in his pocket. So, they're going to be moving on him tonight. Can you get out of there before shit goes down?"

"I'll do my best. Got to stop by Mac's cottage fir—"

Allie cut him off midsentence. "Ethan, if you want to do something useful, tell this asshole to go to the hospital. He's been shot and is bleeding out while you two bullshit."

Trever glared at her. "It's not that bad."

"Trever, you're still recovering, you can't afford—" The concern in Ethan's voice echoed through the truck.

"Enough!" he snapped. Everyone was running off at the mouth and it was beginning to piss him off. Or maybe it was the fact that the secrets he wanted to stay buried kept coming out into the open. "I'm fine, Allie's fine. I'll let you know when we reach Chicago."

"You're not fine."

"Allie…" His features softened as he registered the fear in her eyes. "I'll stitch myself up. We're not far from the cottage. It's going to be fine."

"Allyson," Ethan cut in before she could argue. "Just keep pressure on the wound and him conscious until he can patch himself up. If he passes out, call me. I'll find a doctor in the area that will patch him up without calling the authorities."

"A lot of help you are."

"Sounds like you've got your hands full but, Trever, I'm trusting you to keep her safe." With that, the line went dead.

"Bastard," Allie grumbled.

"You know you love him, even though he sent me instead of coming himself." Trever dropped the phone onto his lap.

And damn if I'm not happy I'm the one that's here to protect you.

His sweet Allie still had an anger streak a mile wide, and this time it was focused directly at him.

Chapter Five

Doubts

The words *he sent me* kept circling in Allyson's thoughts, clawing at her stomach. He wasn't there because he heard she was in trouble and wanted to protect her. He was there because she was his latest mission. It wasn't the first time he said Ethan sent him, but it was the first time those words sunk in.

Why would I, even for a moment, think he came back because he made a mistake? That he still loved me even after all these years?

The miles sped past until Trever turned onto a dirt road. The first tear slipped past Allyson's guard to silently roll down her cheek. It was all taking its toll and she had finally had enough. All she wanted was a good night's sleep and to wake up the next morning with this all being a terrible dream. None of this was real. She couldn't be this deep in a pile of shit when all she'd done was go to the store. She couldn't have lost her brother due to drugs. If none of that had happened Trever wouldn't have stroll back into her life looking better than he did the last time she'd seen him.

"Come on, Allie, I'm going to be okay. Don't cry, baby."

"Don't call me that!" She pressed against the gauze to emphasize her point. Childish, yes, but she wanted him to hurt as much as she did.

"Wo...owww!" His wow turned into a groan of pain at her pressing hard on his wound.

"He sent you. You don't want to be here, so why don't you leave? I'll be fine on my own."

"What are you talking about?" Trever pulled the truck to a stop outside the cottage and shoved it in park. "I'm not leaving you."

"Because then you've failed the mission," she spat at him and removed her hands from the bloody bandages to climb out of the truck.

"Wait, Allie."

"No, Trever, I can't do this. Call Ethan, have him replace you with someone else. I'm done." She hopped down onto the ground and slammed the door. She needed a minute and some air. Each breath felt like swallowing a mouthful of glass and burned her lungs, but it wasn't the air, it was her heart that was breaking again.

My little romantic…don't ever give up on that dream. One day, baby girl, your Prince Charming will sweep you off your feet. Ask Mama, she'll tell you I did just that. Her dad's words echoed through her mind.

"You were wrong, Daddy. Prince Charming doesn't exist."

She didn't remember climbing the porch steps but a few minutes later she realized she was gently swinging on the porch swing and Trever was standing before her.

"We need to talk."

"Please, Trever, not now." She rubbed her arms, trying to chase the goosebumps away, not sure if they were from her emotions or the breeze that was picking up.

He grabbed hold of her wrists, pulling them out toward him. "You're going to get blood all over you."

She stared down at her hands and for the first time she noticed the blood coating them. *His blood.* He was bleeding because of her. Her brother dragged her into this and now she was dragging him and Ethan down with her.

"I can't…you don't deserve this."

"Come on, let's get you cleaned up." Trever gently pulled her up and wrapped his arm around her shoulder.

"I've got to go back. I have to face this and make it right." She barely noticed as he led her through the cottage toward a bathroom. "I can't let others get hurt because of me."

In the bathroom, he lifted her up onto the counter and went to work on cleaning her hands. Allyson sat there only somewhat aware of what was happening. Over and over she mumbled to herself, not really making sense even to herself, but it almost sounded like she had some sort of plan. Something that would allow her to protect those around her.

"I'm sorry, I shouldn't have dragged you or Ethan or anyone else into this. It's not that simple. I just can't leave. They'll find me…kill me…"

"Enough." He gripped her shoulders. "Look at me, Allie."

"My fault—"

He placed his finger under her chin and gently tipped her head back until she was looking at him. "I'm going to get you through this. I know you don't believe my promises anymore but you have my word on this."

"I shouldn't have dragged you into this." *Damn you, Anthony!* Tears filled her vision again as the images of what had happened flashed before her.

"You still haven't told me how you got into this situation. And you know what? It doesn't really matter because I'm going to get you out of it."

"Anthony…" Her chest tightened when she said her brother's name. "I need a minute. I feel like I'm falling apart."

"Why don't you go lie down on the sofa for a few minutes? I'll patch myself up and then we can talk."

Not trusting her voice, she nodded and hopped off the counter. A few minutes were all she needed and she could pull herself together. She had to, there was no other option. When Trever walked out of her life before, a piece of her broke. Now he'd strolled back in right after her brother was murdered and she was losing her sanity. The SEALs would call him back and he'd exit her life as quickly as he'd entered. Even knowing that, she didn't want him to get hurt because of her. Trever was still a SEAL. He wasn't going to stay. When he left again, he'd break her heart just as he had the last time.

She walked past the sofa and out the front door. The cool wind whipped her hair into her face, reminding her a storm was coming. It would blow in quickly and when it left it would be hotter than before. She needed to make it back to the main road before the storm hit and hitch a ride. She'd head back from where they came and hope she could live long enough to meet the one who was in charge, the one who was sending his men after her. If she only had a moment of his time maybe she could offer herself in place of anyone else getting hurt. She'd do that to protect Trever, who was now on this guy's radar after killing two of his men.

Jogging down the dirt road she tried to remember what Anthony had called him. "Venison?" She shook her head; that wasn't right. "Venni? No, damn it, think."

"I got to see Vezio...Steel..." The words Anthony said as they climbed into the car after shopping whispered through her mind as if he was right there.

"Vezio Persichetti. Steel. That's who I need to find."

"Going somewhere?" Trever hollered out the window of his truck.

"Damn it." Her heart pounded in her chest. Lost in her thoughts, she hadn't heard the truck come up alongside her. She glanced over at him to find him with his famous cocky grin, making her want to reach in the window and wipe it off his face. The stupid grin always made her weak in the knees, and she'd have rather seen any look on his face but that. Because it meant he wasn't about to give up and let her handle this by herself. If only she'd gotten to the main road before he caught up with her, she might have been able to lose him.

"Get in."

"No!" she hollered back, picking up her pace.

Instead of arguing, Trever gunned the truck forward and turned it sideways, sending dust flying through the air and blocking the road. He jumped out of the truck and came around it to stand near the passenger door. "We can do this one of two ways. Now get in the truck."

"Fuck you, Trever. You don't get to tell me what to do after all these years. I'm not one of your lackeys you can order around."

The overgrown brush along the sides of the road would make for an interesting journey, but she'd make it through if he was determined to continue blocking the way.

"This is crazy and you know it. You go back and you'll get yourself killed. I'm not letting that happen."

"If I don't then he'll come after you."

The thought of Trever dead was nauseating. Through a broken heart, years alone, and all the worry about him overseas fighting for his country, she still loved him. She wasn't about to see him hurt because of her.

"Let him." He shrugged, clearly not the least bit worried. "Do you really think I can't handle myself against a drug dealer? I've gone up against worse people than him."

"He's not just a drug dealer, he's a gangster. He's Vezio Persichetti. Everyone calls him Steel."

"Interesting name for a gangster."

"He goes by that name since he prefers to use a steel crowbar on people. Anthony said he likes to get bloody and set an example of what happens when you go against him." Speaking the words aloud was worse than them running through her thoughts. They were real now. The thought of him using the crowbar on her and the pain that would come with it made her stomach heave.

"You think you can reason with someone like him?"

The monotone of his voice was grinding against her, as well as his *I don't care* attitude. He was trying too hard to appear as if he didn't care. That alone made her wonder if he still had some feelings for her. Or was all this because of Ethan? It was beginning to play havoc on her emotions.

She took a deep breath. "Look, Trever, this is my fight. I called Ethan when I was scared but it was wrong for me to call. It's even worse that he dragged you into this. You've already gotten shot twice and had to kill...enough is enough. Let's just go our separate ways."

"Not a chance. Now get into the truck. We have some things to discuss back at the cottage."

Growling, she stomped over to him. She wanted to smack him, but the sight of blood still coating his chest stopped her. "Trever, you're like a dog with a bone. But I'm not a mission to set this right. You're not going to fail if we go our separate ways. So please just stop."

"Do I have to pick you up and put you in the truck myself?" His arms uncrossed from his chest and he stepped forward. "Because I will."

"You're hurt."

"I will survive. *Now get in the truck.*" His voice raised slightly with the last part, the order crystal clear, yet still she didn't move. "By morning, Steel will no longer be a problem."

"What?"

"Get in and I'll explain." He pulled open the passenger door. "Then if you want to go our separate ways I'll take you wherever you want to go once he's taken care of. If you want to stay with Ethan until things cool down, I'll see you to Montana. The decision will be yours. First we have things to discuss and we're not doing them out here in the open."

Reluctantly she got into the truck. "I'm holding you to what you said and you will take me back home tomorrow."

"Whatever you want." He nodded and shut the door.

"That sounded like sarcasm," she mumbled to the empty truck. *I can't believe I gave into him again. How am I ever going to distance myself if I keep letting him smooth talk me?*

Chapter Five

Her Brother

"I can't keep doing this. I've got to get away from him or I'm going to end up with my heart broken again." Allyson mumbled to herself as Trever strolled around the front of the truck.

Let him keep you safe so you don't end up like me. Swearing she could hear Anthony's voice she spun around to look at the back seat. The seat was empty, making her question her sanity. "Great, now I'm losing my fucking mind. Hearing shit that isn't there."

"Huh?" Trever asked, climbing into the driver's seat and shifting the idling truck into drive.

"Nothing, just losing the last bit of sanity I have."

"Oh, well then, that's nothing to worry about." He chuckled, shooting the truck quickly up the dirt road back toward the cottage. "You were never very sane."

"I lived life on my own terms, doing what I wanted. That doesn't mean I was insane. I just—"

"Had a death wish?" he offered. "You were sixteen when you hopped on Lightning. Bigger men have tried to ride that bull and were bucked off before they even began. There you are. Shit, I thought your daddy was going to have a heart attack. He was pissed and who got the blame? Not his precious little girl, but me and Anthony. We should have been watching his little girl and stopped you."

"Hey, I did just fine on Lightning. Not a broken bone or even a scratch. He was a baby." Even as she said it, she remembered how scared she had been when she climbed onto the back of the bucking bull. Moments before she decided to give into her wild side, she'd witnessed one of the ranch hands get torn up for being in the same pen. Yet that didn't stop her. She hoped onto the bull's back. It was a hell of a ride and an adrenaline rush like no other.

Anthony had been livid with her when she stepped out of Lightning's pen, hollering at her about how she could have gotten herself killed. At first, she figured he was only angry with her because their father had lashed out at him. Later, after Trever had left, Anthony cornered her on her way out of the bathroom.

"You're my little sister," he'd said. *"I'm supposed to protect you, but when you rush off and do crazy things like today you make my job hard. You weigh, what, ninety-five pounds? I've seen that bull trample a man nearly to death who was twice your size."*

"You're only mad because Daddy yelled at you." She stepped past him on her way back to her bedroom.

He grabbed her arm before she could get out of reach. "Is it so hard to believe I care about you?"

"Maybe." There was something in the way he looked at her that told her he was telling the truth. "Fine, I'm sorry, but it was fun."

"You have to be careful. Lightning is a beast and he won't think twice about stomping you just because you're a girl." He let go of her arm but didn't move back. "One more thing…watch out for Trever."

"What? Your best friend Trever? What is there to worry about when it comes to him?" Anthony and Trever had been friends for more than ten years. All the time she had lusted after him while he never saw her as anything more than Anthony's little sister. They were less

36

than two years apart, but at sixteen and eighteen that seemed like a world of difference.

"I saw how he looked at you today…just be careful. I'd hate to have to beat his ass for hurting my baby sis."

Her protective older brother was right. Two weeks later things changed between her and Trever and they happened fast. *I miss the brother you were, Anthony.*

"Allie…" Trever stood holding her door open waiting for her to exit the truck.

"Sorry," she mumbled as she stepped out of the truck, her thoughts of the past disappearing like a popped bubble. "I was thinking about the day I rode Lightning."

"Anthony was livid. I doubt you saw it because you were so in the moment, but I had to stop him from climbing over the fence and getting himself killed to get you off that bull." They made their way into the house and he grabbed the rag that was tossed on the counter, most likely when he realized she was gone.

"We had some words later that night." She shoved her hands into the pockets of her jeans. "He was the best big brother I could have asked for. Even after he got messed up, he was always there when I needed him."

"How long ago did this start? When did he get hooked on drugs?" When she stood there with her mouth open he added, "I figured if you were there getting drugs, it had to be for him, and from the way you're talking I'm going to assume you know he's dead. Not that he was captured by them."

She stepped back until the back of her legs brushed against the sofa. "Two…" Her voice broke and she forced herself to sit down. "Two years ago, he started using but he's been tangled up with Steel and his gang longer than that."

"How long?" he pressed.

"A year after you joined the Navy things started to change. He withdrew from the family and would sleep the day away. Dad put up with it for a couple months before he kicked him out. That's when he fell in with Steel. He started out selling, but somewhere along the line it was too tempting and he experimented with the products he was selling."

"So, was he buying when you found yourselves in trouble?"

"I think that's what he intended, but it didn't go down like that." She thought back to how it all started and could see herself sitting behind the wheel of her car, the passenger window rolled down allowing her to hear everything being said despite something telling her to keep her gaze straight ahead.

"Come on, Steel, I'm good for it. I'll get the money and will handle your next problem no cost."

"You hear this, Legs? He'll handle my next problem, no cost." Steel's voice stayed light, almost joking.

"He's the problem and I'm about to deal with him," Legs replied, his voice full of excitement.

"Come on guys." There was an edge to Anthony's voice she hadn't heard before making her turn toward him.

"Fucking grifter, thinks he can outsmart me." Steel grabbed Anthony's collar, pushing him against the building. *"We know you've been stealing from me, using the product for your own recreational uses. Trying to sell inferior products to our customers to come up with the money that you owe me."*

"Don't do anything stupid," Anthony pleaded. *"I'll get you the money."* Anthony held his hands up by his head and did nothing to fight back. *"Come on, I just need a fix."*

"You're going to need a lot more than that." Steel reached into his suit jacket and pulled out a gun, the silencer already in place.

Allyson wanted to scream, to warn Anthony, but it all happened so fast. One moment she saw the gun and the next he lay dead in the alleyway, a hole right between his eyes, blood and brain matter seeping out onto the concrete. She must have made a sound, because they turned to her. With a tip of Steel's head, the other man, Legs, was coming toward her.

"No! Please no…"

"Shh, Allie." Trever sat down beside her, his arm around her shoulders. "It's okay, sweetie."

She leaned against him, her body shaking with grief and fear. Her brother was dead, killed before her very eyes, and now they were after her. Her life had been mundane, normal. She had never even been pulled over for speeding, and now she found herself hunted by criminals. She wanted a do over. To go to the grocery store, get what they needed, and tell Anthony she wasn't taking him to see Steel. If she could do that, then it would all be okay. It would have all been some horrible nightmare.

"He needed a fix, but he owed Steel money." Needing the support, she clung to him. "They killed him…now they're after me."

"It's going to be okay."

"How? They're never going to stop. It's not some corner drug dealer. This is organized. Steel runs it locally, but there have to be others above him, and there are certainly others below him. He sent men after me. They caught me once, and I wouldn't have escaped except one was young, he was new, and took pity on me. When they stopped to get gas, he opened the trunk to check on me. I bashed him in the head with a lead pipe and ran. Otherwise I'd be dead already and this would be over." She wiped the tears off her cheeks and took a couple of deep breaths. "I just want it over."

Chapter Six

Reconnecting

The needle pierced Trever's skin, then he tugged the stitch tight. It was hard stitching his own back, but since Allie had finally calmed down, he hadn't wanted to bother her by asking for her help. Blood loss was already starting to affect him with a touch of lightheadedness and his pulse was weaker. He needed to get himself stitched up and the bleeding stopped before he was no good to her.

"You should have done this already."

He turned to find her standing near the bathroom door, her face pale, and a blanket loosely wrapped around her shoulders. "I started to."

"Then you stopped when you heard me leave?"

"Close, but I didn't actually hear you leave. I went to find you to help me clean the exit wound. It's hard to do it when it's on your back. Looking into the mirror and trying to do it is complicated. I screw up and start to put the needle in the wrong area because everything is backward." He grinned.

"Let me help." She shrugged off the blanket, letting it fall on the hall floor, and stepped into the snug bathroom.

"You don't even know what you're doing."

"Before Mom died we used to make handstitched quilts. She'd take some of the blankets to the local hospital for the newborn babies and the others to a nursing home for their residents. I think I can remember how to put of line of stitches in." She hopped up onto the counter, allowing her a better view of the wound and held out her hand for the needle. "Have you taken something for the pain?"

"I'm fine."

"Oh right, a big Navy SEAL like you doesn't need something to dull the pain like us mere mortals." She spread her legs and grabbed the back belt loop of his jeans, gently pulling him back between them.

"Nothing like that, smart ass. I need my mind to be clear, which means no drugs, no alcohol. So just do it." Her fingers brushed against his skin and he could feel her hesitate. "You can do it."

"Why don't you give me your gun and take something? I can handle keeping us safe until the pill wears off. I don't want to hurt you."

"Allie, either you do it or I will. I've lost enough blood already; this needs to be closed up." Her fingers brushed along the sides of the hole, pressing in enough she could push the skin together to stitch it up, and the pain was enough to have him sucking in a deep breath.

"How many times have you had to stitch yourself up?"

"A time or two." Stars danced in his vision as the skin was tugged with each stitch.

"Almost done. Do you need a break?"

"Finish it," He bit out through clenched teeth, cursing himself for letting her see the pain he was in.

Each second that passed felt like a whole minute, and when she knotted the string he let out a deep sigh. His body stayed stiff and every part of him hurt, yet all he wanted to do was turn around and wrap his arms around her. He'd have taken a hundred more rounds if it meant keeping her safe.

Ignoring the blood, she rubbed her hands over his back, teasing along his other scars, seeing some of what had happened to him over the years. The tender caresses brought the part of him alive that he'd closed off when he left her. It was freeing, giving him a new lease on life.

He turned around to face her. "Fuck, Allie." Before he could think it through, his hand was tangled in her hair, bringing her head forward as he leaned down to kiss her. His lips claimed hers with all the heat and desire that had been building in him over the years. He sucked her bottom lip gently between his teeth, nipping it lightly until she opened her lips and let him in. A soft moan escaped her as his tongue explored the contours of her mouth.

"Ahh…"

With another quick peck, he pulled back enough to look at her. "I want you, Allie."

"Oh, Trever…" She ran her hand up his chest, her gaze glued to his. "I've never been so scared as I was hiding in that bathroom. The thought of you dead…"

"We're both okay." He understood what she meant. When the bullet tore through his shoulder, the pain exploded through his body and darkness threatened to close in around him, his only thought was if he went down before he took those bastards out, she'd be in danger. It kept him going. She kept him going. Just as she had while he was overseas. The memories of her reminded him what he was fighting for and why he was trying to make the world a better and safer place.

"If I'm going to die—"

"You're not. I told you I'm going to fix this."

"Fine, but that still means you're…" She shook her head. "Screw it. Trever, I want you, one last time."

"Just one more time?" He kissed along her jawline until he reached the sweet spot below her ear. Grazing his teeth over the area, he blew his cool breath against her flushed skin. "I'll have to make you reconsider that because I have plans for more than just one time." He tugged her tank top up her body until she grabbed the hem of it and pulled it over her head, dropping it on the floor.

"You're leaving—" She moaned in pleasure as he nibbled and kissed his way down to her breasts. "Over the years I can't tell you how often I've thought of this. Of you."

He slid his hand around her body, quickly finding the clasp of her bra and unhooking it. The material slid down her arms, revealing her perky breasts, making his shaft strain against his jeans and press against the counter. Her words *you're leaving* barely registered in the fog of desire. *Where was he going?* He couldn't remember. All he knew is he wanted her there with him wherever he went. He'd made a mistake before and he was going to prove that he was worthy of her.

Claiming her nipple with his teeth, he gently tugged, making it hard before moving over to the other one. Without breaking contact, he unhooked her jeans. "We should be doing this in the bedroom."

"The bedroom is overrated." She rose up, tugging her tight jeans down the curve of her butt. "Back up and let me get out of these."

He stepped back, giving her space to kick off her shoes and jeans while he took care of his own clothes. In a flash they were naked and he closed the distance between them.

"Gorgeous. Damn Allie. The memory of you I have burned into my brain doesn't do you justice." He gripped her hips, easing her toward the edge of the counter, crushed his mouth to hers, and slid his hand between her legs. Unerringly finding her core, he thrust his fingers into her and she moaned around his unrelenting kiss. He held her captive against his body, teasing her clit with his thumb. Fierce desire had her rocking against his hand. She was ready for him.

"I want you," she murmured against his mouth, her nails digging into his sides as she arched into him.

His teeth grazed her lower lip and he pulled his hand away. Her cries of frustration only confirmed the climax he felt building within her, but he ignored her demands.

"My sweet Allie, how long has it been? Surely you haven't been waiting all this time for me," he teased.

"You cocky bastard, you'd like that, wouldn't you? Keep messing with me and I'll leave you high and dry." She grabbed his hips. "I've gone through Hell. Don't you think I've earned this release?"

"Humm, I guess orgasming is a good way to relive stress." Trever adjusted his angle, gliding his shaft over her opening, pulling a moan from her. Slowly he glided the length of him in, just a little at first, her nails digging into his back as he worked his way inside her tight passage. Halfway in he stopped and slid out, even as she clung to him trying to force him to stay.

Once he was out, he gripped her hips and slammed his length into her, filling her completely. He didn't give her time to catch her breath and began rocking their bodies back and forth, each thrust gaining momentum.

He left her mouth and kissed a path to her neck. She pressed herself tighter against him, matching him thrust for thrust until she was bouncing off the counter. He quickly adjusted, sliding one hand under her butt, lifted her, and spun around to press her against the wall. With her secured between his body and the wall, she wrapped her legs around his hips, the heel of her foot digging into him so he couldn't pull back too far. Rather than pulling away, each thrust was faster and deeper than the last.

In this position, her chest was pressed against his and he lost the view of her breasts bouncing as he thrusted into her. A small price to pay to have himself buried deep within her, but he'd remember it next time. He longed to claim her nipple with his mouth, to tug it between his teeth as he hammered himself into her.

"Trever!" she cried out, her nails clawing into his shoulders, careful of his wounds.

Tension had her muscles constricting around him as her orgasm neared. She leaned into him, every pump of his hips sending pulses of pleasure exploding through him. In his arms, she came apart at the seams as her climax rippled through her and he continued to drive into her, her moans echoing off the walls. He pushed into her again before his own ecstasy had him exploding within her. His moans mixed with hers until he dropped his head into the curve of her shoulder, planting gentle kisses along the nape of her neck.

"Wow." Her voice was low as she tried to regain her breath. "That was…"

"Amazing? The best you ever had?" he offered, lifting his head to look at her.

"Okay." Her lips curled up into a smug smirk. "'Cause you know it would have been better if you hadn't been shot and covered in dried blood."

"Oh, really now? Well give me a couple of days to heal this bullet hole that I took for you and I'll show you how amazing it can be."

"Took for me?" She slapped his ass, making him arch into her and forcing a moan from between her lips as his cock shot deeper within her. "My daddy always said you should move out of the way of speeding bullets. Guess you never learned that lesson. I'd have thought the SEALs would have taught you a thing or two about it. Well maybe next training they'll go over that."

Trever slid out of her and helped her stand before stepping back. "There won't be a next one."

"What?"

"I'm out." Unable to handle it if he saw disappointment in her eyes, he leaned down and grabbed the discarded clothes from the floor.

"Out? What do you mean out? Out of here?"

He tossed the clothes onto the counter. "I'm no longer a SEAL." Those words ripped through him worse than the bullet had. All the years he'd trained to be a SEAL, only for it to all end with one injury. "I was injured overseas and that's it."

"That's where the scars came from?" She reached out and her hand brushed over his chest before he stepped back. "What happened?"

"This is not a conversation I want to have, especially not naked." He wanted to shower, but he grabbed his jeans and tugged them on.

"What, you don't want to talk about it so you shut me out?" Pain laced within her words.

"What do you want me to say?" His voice rose. He didn't want to talk about it because it meant he failed. He failed himself, his team, and most importantly, her.

"You're shutting me out, just like last time." She snatched her clothes.

"What?" Now he was the one confused. "What do you mean like last time?"

"You joined the Navy, promising me everything would be fine. You'd do boot camp and you said when you were through I could join you. Maybe I was young and gullible, but I thought we'd get married because you know Daddy would have never allowed me to move in with you otherwise. What happened?" She paused for a moment before continuing. "You joined the SEALs, and when I finally saw you, your parting words were: *I can't promise you forever and you deserve that.* You didn't give me a say in any of it. You shut me out and tossed me aside. I'm not going to stand by and let you do that again."

And every day since then I've regretted that decision. Instead of telling her that, Trever kept his mouth shut as she stormed past him.

"I need to shower," Trever said.

"So? I'm not stopping you." She stood in the hall, her clothes pressed against her chest, but she wouldn't meet his gaze.

"Do I need to tie you to the bed? Because I brought handcuffs if I need them. Or are you going to be here when I get out?"

"I bet you'd just love to use them. Keep me tied to the bed, so you could have your pleasures while keeping me out of the things that matter." She shook her head. "Don't worry. I'll be here because it's getting dark and I'm not rushing off with a storm coming. Tomorrow you'll take me back home. You want to keep me at arm's length; then we'll go our separate ways."

"Allie..." he called after her but she continued down the hall toward the living room. He'd screwed things up again and he had no idea how to make them right. He kept his voice low enough that she wouldn't hear him. "I fucking love you, Allyson Marie Mason. I always have."

Chapter Seven

Past and Future Collide

Lightning lit the night sky, followed a moment later by the loud rumblings of thunder. Allyson sat on the window seat, her tears flowing as freely as the rain fell from the clouds. The storm raged on as if matching the turmoil of her emotions. She had given into her desires and had sex with Trever only to have her heart torn out again. Why had she thought things would be different? He had locked her out of his decision to join the SEALs and had ended what they had between them. Now he was doing the same thing, only in a different way. She would not stand by and let someone make the decisions that affected her life without her even having a say.

She rested her head against the pane of glass and stared off into the darkness. Someone could be watching hidden within the trees and she wouldn't even know until it was too late. Although she didn't want to die, she didn't have the energy to move away from the window. She felt broken, as if Trever had torn something out of her and left her with nothing.

I guess he did...my heart.

She hadn't been paying attention to her surroundings and hadn't realized Trever had come into the living room, let alone that he was only steps away, until he spoke, startling her.

"It was a night like this and I found peace in the raging storm. I was listening to the rain beat against the Humvee on our way back to the helicopter rendezvous point." Trever leaned against the far side of the window frame, his gaze on something outside and not looking at her. "Everything about it was routine. That should have been suspicious by itself, but we were all just thankful for a quiet night. Too many were injured or killed…we were ready to come home. We ran over an IED, and next thing I knew I was airborne. The Humvee was in flames, pieces were flying through the air. Then everything went dark. That's all I remember until I woke up in the hospital bed."

She sat there for a moment waiting for him to continue but he remained silent, forcing her to ask. "How bad were you injured? Is that what the scars are from?"

"Some." He ran his hand through his still wet hair, sending droplets down his shirt. "I was unconscious because of the swelling around my brain. Some of the doctors believed if I woke up at all I would never regain the ability to talk, or walk, or basically take care of myself. I guess everyone was split on what my condition would be if I regained consciousness. When I came around, I was weak, though thankfully I didn't have any lasting effects. At least that's what I thought at the time."

This time when he stopped, she waited him out because she knew it wasn't over. There was more to his story and he'd get to it at his own pace. She reached up and took his hand, gently pulling him down onto the window seat next to her.

"I suffered a brain injury. There's some stupid medical lingo for it, but it doesn't really matter. I have migraines now. They steal my thoughts and threaten to send me into a world of darkness when my eyesight goes dim. They've gotten better and will continue to, but it's why I've been medically discharged from the Navy. Ethan convinced Lucas that they needed me to join Safety First Security in Montana. I haven't taken agreed to the position yet, but even they don't know the extent of my migraines. If they did, they wouldn't offer me the job. I've failed."

"You haven't." She scooted closer to him, keeping his hand in hers. "You fought to stay alive. That's not failing."

"I've failed my team by being medically discharged. I fail myself because I should have been able to beat this and get back to my duty. Most importantly, I failed you."

"How?" Her brows knitted together in confusion.

"I threw away what we had because I thought I could do more with the SEALs than as a Navy sailor and I didn't want to put you through the stress of the job. The never knowing where I was or when I'd be back. Classified assignments one after another until you weren't sure if you were married to a myth and then I'd pop home for a week or two before leaving again. That was no life for you. I threw it all away and then I didn't even make it."

"Bullshit, Trever. You did your duty, you served your country, and you made it home. You didn't fail anyone, and you sure as hell didn't fail me." She rose up, swung her leg over his waist, and straddled him so they were face to face, giving him no option but to look at her. "I'm the last one you have to worry about failing because all I wanted was for you to make it home safe. You did that. I didn't ask for anything more. I didn't ask for you to come back to me when you did. I just wanted you alive and safe. To be here with you right now is more than I could have ever hoped for."

"You don't get it." He hung his head. "This is what I've worked for all these years, it's what I know how to do. If I can't work for Safety First Security what am I supposed to do?"

"You'll find something." She reached up and cupped the sides of his face. "You seem okay to me. How bad are the migraines? Any other lasting effects?"

"They're nothing to worry about."

She dropped her hands away as he started to build his walls again, shutting her out.

"Fine." She tried to keep the pain out of her voice but it bothered her that he was closing her out again. It shouldn't have because he wasn't going to stay but it did. No matter how things went, their time together was temporary.

"I'm sorry." He took her hand and stopped her when she started to climb off him. "Deny that there's anything wrong and it will go away. Isn't that how it's supposed to work? It didn't; the doctors saw right through it. I guess even a SEAL can't hide it when the migraine steals his vision or when even the slightest bit of light seems like a firework going off in front of their eyes."

"How often?" Allyson asked.

In the back of her mind she wondered what would happen if they found themselves in the same situation as they did back at the motel but with him having one of those migraines. Even though that was a concern, she was more worried about him in general. What if one came when he was alone on a job? Was there brain damage that was causing this?

"More than I care for. Don't worry, Allie, I'm okay."

"Sure, just some brain injury that now leaves you with disabling migraines. Nothing to worry about." She shook her head. "What's so bad about me worrying about you? We were in love; those feelings don't just go away…"

Hell, I'm still in love with you, you big dope.

"It's called post-concussion syndrome, and in time it will go away. In some people it lasts a few weeks or months, while in others a year or more."

She couldn't help but notice that he didn't comment on the part about them being in love and she wasn't sure what to make of that. If he wanted to forget about that period in their lives, then why did they have sex in the bathroom?

This isn't the time to dissect this relationship or the love I still feel for him.

She stayed on topic, pushing for more information before he clammed up again. "How long since your injury?"

"Six months. Everything else is healed but my brain. I've only been officially medically discharged for two weeks. It's an adjustment." He slid his hands over her hips and gently up her sides. "Ethan knows I am having migraines. He knows I'm on medication to ease them and that it's helping. Still I don't know what he's told Lucas or the others who work with Safety First Security. It's something I had planned on discussing with them if I accepted the position."

"You don't even work for them?" Wasn't that why her cousin sent him? He was busy with another assignment and Trever was free or closer. She never asked, only assumed.

"No, not yet. Ethan sent me after you. Well after a woman—"

"Huh?" The more he revealed the more confused she got.

"I was told about the situation and that 'a woman' needed my help, but Ethan didn't tell me it was you." His arms tightened around her waist as if he thought she was going to slip away from him. "I think he thought I wouldn't come if I knew it was you. In reality, I almost turned down the assignment because of the lack of information. I don't like going into situations without at least most of the details."

"I knew you didn't want to be here. I was just an assignment." She tried to pull back from him but he held tight, hugging her closer to his chest.

"Don't. I'm not through." He waited until she quit wiggling. "Even if Ethan hadn't come to me with this, I'd have come to you if I had known you were in trouble."

"Why?"

"Isn't it obvious?" His thumb slipped under the hem of her tank top, teasing along the small of her back.

Her throat tightened and she didn't trust herself enough to speak without her voice breaking, so she shook her head.

"I still love you, Allie. I never stopped. You've always held my heart, even if you didn't know it." He pressed his lips to hers in a soft kiss.

When he walked out of her life, she had waited day after day, expecting him to come back or at least call and tell her it was a mistake. That he loved her and he was wrong about everything. With each day that passed without a word from him, she realized he wasn't coming back. Now, after all the time, he was there before her saying the very words she waited so long to hear. *I love you.* Those three little words melted her heart yet the fear of him leaving again was still burning wild within her.

"You left. 'I can't offer you forever and that's what you deserve'…you said that, not me. Why should I believe you now? Things suddenly change now that you're not an active duty SEAL, but how long until something else comes along? Will Safety First Security be the new SEALs and force you to leave me behind again?" She let her fears take life and come out in words while her heart told her to tell him she loved him too.

His hands stilled for a moment before he nodded. "I wondered where your fighting spirit had gone. Next time though, if it could be directed at someone else I'd prefer that."

"You deserve this and so much more. You broke my heart." The smirk on his face had the anger within her softening a little.

"I know and I'm sorry. Apologizes can't make amends for the pain I caused you and it doesn't glue the heart back together, but I can. Give me a chance. I'm not worthy of you and with these migraines you might be getting more than you bargained for." With his thumb trailing along the hem of her tank top, gently brushing along her skin, he met her gaze. "When I woke in the hospital you were all I could think about. I've always regretted what I did but laying in that hospital bed I realized you were the best thing in my life. You always had my heart, Allie. In my mind I did what I thought was best for you when I left. I didn't want you to be stuck alone worrying about me. I wanted you to have the husband and kids you always dreamed about."

"You thought about me in the hospital because you were alone and wanted someone there." The moment his muscles tightened, and his dark eyes became darker she instantly regretted those words.

"You're wrong. I thought about you every day I was gone. Every leave I had to stop myself from coming back to Texas and telling you how much I needed you in my life. When I woke up weeks after the accident I thought about how different my life could have been if I had stayed in Texas, married you, and took over my father's business. Also, in that moment I knew I did the right thing by letting you go. I was unconscious for weeks. The doctors didn't know if I'd even make it. The ones that believed I'd pull through weren't even sure what my condition would be when I came to. Most of them thought I'd be a fucking vegetable. Tell me, what kind of life would that have been for you? Weeks of sitting by my bedside not sure if I'd wake and if I did, would I still be the man you loved? What about the children we would have had? How good is a father who's never there? You'd have grown to resent me because of my absence."

"You never gave me the choice. You just shut me out."

"We thought it was best for—"

Her eyes widened and she pressed her hand to his chest, pushing him back away from her. "Wait, what? Who's we?"

"Never mind." He swallowed. "I meant to say I."

"Bullshit! If you want me to trust you, then you need to tell me the truth. Otherwise you're wasting your breath." She pulled back from him and this time he didn't stop her.

"Anthony." Her brother's name was barely a whisper as it left his lips.

"What?" She stumbled back away from him. "You talked to my brother about this?"

"He confronted me." He stood up from the window seat and took a step closer to her. "Shit, Allie. I never meant to say that. It's true, but he's fucking dead now and I don't want you to doubt why he did it. He wanted to protect you. We had friends who did the military and we heard all about how most relationships don't work. Some made it worse than it was but the SEALs weren't going to make it a walk in the park for us. You were young and he was looking out for you. The idea of me making you move to Virginia or California where I'd be stationed didn't sit well with him."

"He...he told me it was for the best. That it wouldn't have worked out with you being gone all the time. Do you know what I did?" She chuckled remembering the look on her brother's face as she made her move. "I kicked him in the nuts."

"Oh hell, I leave you and he takes the punishment. Poor guy." He closed the distance between them, backing her up until her butt was pressed against the back of the sofa. "Don't blame him. He was only looking out for you. I'm the one who ended it. I guess in my own way I was trying to protect you too. Taking you away from everything and everyone you knew so I could be gone more times than not didn't seem fair to you."

"Once again, I should have been included in that decision."

"You're right." He intertwined their fingers. "I was wrong. That doesn't mean I ever stopped loving you. You'll get more than you bargained for but give me another chance. We've been brought together again—"

"By Ethan," she reminded him. "My sneaky cousin sent you here because he knew I still had feelings for you. Throw us together with danger surrounding us with the hope I seek comfort in your arms."

"Sweetie, I'll give you comfort and I'll keep you safe. What more could you want?"

True, Ethan had thrown them back together and she would have a few things to say about his conniving ways. Still she couldn't help but see this as a second chance. Trever was back in her life and they could see where things went. Safety First Security operations might take him away from home, but as long as he came back to her they had a chance of making it work. That was as long as he didn't shut her out again.

"You know, Trever, you're still as cocky as you were when you left, but I love you."

Chapter Eight

Tattoo

Trever dropped his cell phone beside him onto the sofa cushion and rubbed his hands over his face. The call to Ethan had been interesting, but it was nothing like the one he made to Lucas. The migraines were an issue and until he got them under control he couldn't take any Safety First Security assignments. He was too big of a risk and it brought too much danger to their clients and other team members if he had an episode in the field. The bright side of it was that Ethan knew a doctor who specialized in post-concussion syndrome with veterans. He'd schedule an appointment when he got back to Montana and see what could be done. It would require a trip to Billings but if this doctor could help it would be worth the expense. There was a new medication on the market that had been successful with others; maybe it would be with him too.

"So how did it go?" Allie strolled toward him carrying two mugs of hot coffee.

"Pretty much like I expected. I'm a liability and need to get the migraines under control before beginning field assignments. In the meantime, there's some stuff I can do with Safety First Security while I'm waiting to get in to the doctor and start this new medication." He took the coffee from her. "How do you feel about living in Montana?"

"There's nothing left for me here in Texas, so it's the perfect time to start over in a new city. Maybe they won't find me there. Anyways, I told you things would work out." She sat down next to him. "What about Ethan? How did he take the decision to stay in Texas tonight?"

"Like you expected." He set the mug aside and wrapped his uninjured arm around her. "He doesn't like that I'm keeping you here. As he put it, I'm allowing you to stay in the field of danger. He wanted to send us backup, but I told him we were fine. Unless you want another bodyguard?"

"I think my body is guarded enough." She snuggled against him. "So tomorrow…"

"We'll get the call once Vezio has been taken into custody and I'll go see him tomorrow. They already have a strong case against him for other crimes. I'll deliver the warning that if he doesn't call off his men you'll testify against him as well. Then he's looking at murder charges and possibly attempted murder for his attempts on your life. As long as there are no other attempts on your life then what you saw will go no further than between us."

"I hate not getting Anthony justice. Vezio should go down for his murder."

"I know." He kissed her temple. His sweet Allie believed deeply in an eye for an eye. She no doubt wanted to lock Vezio in a cell, pumping him with heroin every day until he was hooked, then stop, wait until he was going out of his mind needing a fix, and then finish him off just like Anthony had been. To her that would have been justice. Her idea of justice was not for Vezio to spend the rest of his life in prison. "Anthony would rather you be safe than for him to have justice. You know that, right?"

"Yeah but…" She shook her head. "It's fine. At least if this works I'll be able to give him a funeral."

"But you'll have no reason to stay in Montana."

"Really?" She tipped her head back and looked up at him. "Here I thought

I had a different reason."

"What's that?"

"You." She pushed her elbow lightly into his stomach. "Maybe you'd rather I stay here?"

"Oh no, you're coming with me, you already said it. What about your father's ranch?"

"You didn't hear?" She took a drink of her coffee and then set it aside. "We lost it after he died. That was almost a year ago now."

"What happened?"

"Between Anthony stealing from the ranch and Dad trying to bail him out of trouble it was going under quick." She shook her head, trying not to blame Dad for trying to save his son from the hold drugs had on him. Dad expected Anthony to take over the ranch, but that had been a lost cause. "When Dad got sick and then passed away I had to sell off the ranch to pay the bills. Even after everything, I stood by Anthony and tried to get him to clean up his life. For about a month after Dad's funeral, Anthony cleaned up his act. I thought he could overcome it. I got a small apartment and picked up more bookkeeping jobs."

"We talked occasionally, but we drifted apart over the years. I knew he was experimenting, but I didn't realize he was that deep into drugs." He squeezed her tight against him. "Seems like nothing went as we planned. Anthony always said he was going to take over the ranch."

"You were going to take over your dad's business."

"Well Patrick did that, and did more than I could have ever imagined." He let out a deep laugh. "He's the reason I was able to get here so quickly."

"How's that?"

"Patrick was in Montana for a business meeting and I told him I needed to borrow his plane to come save a woman in distress back in our hometown. He was pissed when I wouldn't give him any more information, but he didn't know that *I* didn't even know who I was going to find when I arrived in Texas. Being the gentleman he is who would stop to help anyone in need, he ordered his pilot to take me anywhere I needed to go. Now when we're done here we've got to make a pit stop in Chicago and personally thank him. Then he'll know I didn't make it all up to hitch a ride on his private plane."

"Chicago?"

"Yeah, he's made it big. He took over Alexander Cattle and started distributing it worldwide, along with partnering farms. A couple years ago, he hired a full-time manager for the Texas ranch and moved to Chicago to have a bigger hand in the distributing, to grow it, and bring on more farms. I thought it was a weird place to be when you're working with farms but he's done everything he hoped for and more."

"Let's go to bed." She ran her hand down his leg. "I think there's more that you can do for me."

He rose, stepped in front of her, and pulled her up until she was pressed against his chest. "The night is young and we have all night. Let's make good use of it."

They made it across the living room to the bedroom, their clothes being tugged off as they went, dropping were they fell. Naked before they made it to the bed, he climbed onto it to lay in the center. "Come here."

Allyson hesitantly climbed onto the bed and he grabbed her hips, pulling her on top of him until she was straddling his waist. Her hands went to his chest, her fingers teased along the curves of his muscles before moving along the scars on his chest. The touch was sweet and had his shaft hardening at the gentleness of it all. He had tried to keep his scars hidden, because they were a reminder of the shit he'd been through.

"Your tattoo..." She traced her finger along the design of the owl stretching across his chest. "There's something written on his feathers."

"Yes." He closed his eyes as her finger caressed along the outline of the owl. From a distance the meaning was hidden but if the light was better she'd had seen what he had added within the tattoo. He never shared the meaning of his tattoo with anyone, at least not until now. "It's names of those I knew who were killed in action. I wanted something that honored them and I came up with it when I was drunk one night. Owl was my call sign so it made sense to add their names within it. The feathers are jagged representing their life being cut short."

"So much death."

"That's the cost of war. It gives us freedom, safety, and protects the ones we love back home." The words made it sound like he didn't care, though that wasn't true. "We all know the cost when we sign up and some of us pay it with our blood and our lives. None of us would ever step back and say, oh no forget this, I'm not ready to die. Because you know what? It doesn't matter where you are or how old you are, when your time is up it's up. Live life to the fullest every day so you'll never regret a moment of life when it's your time."

"You've grown wise beyond your years." She leaned down, hovering above his face, her hair falling around her. "No regrets...I can do that."

"It's easier said than done." He ran his hands up her naked back. "You've always been my one...the one regret that I walked away from."

"You're back, and that's what matters. Now we have to make up for lost time."

"Well what are we waiting for then?" He gave her ass a light tap. "I want to be inside of you."

"Maybe I'm not ready," She teased, leaning back so his shaft brushed against her slit. "Foreplay—"

Her words were cut off with a gasp when he adjusted slightly and slid his shaft into her opening. "Is important, but right now we both need this. You want this as much as I do."

"Is that so?" Her voice hitched up a notch as he worked himself deeper into her.

"Well if you don't…" He slid out of her and let the tip of his shaft brush against her clit.

"Don't you dare!" Her hand landed firmly on his chest. "Trever…"

"See what I mean?" He lifted her hips slightly to give him the access he needed. His gaze met hers as he teased his finger along her most sensitive parts.

"Now, Trever," she demanded.

He slid his shaft into her warm, wet core, his manhood filling her completely, pushing back inside of her with such force that she raked her nails over his chest and moaned his name. With every thrust, his pace sped. Stroke after stroke, the tempo between them intensified until his hips where slamming into hers, a driving force with each pump of his hips. The thrusts became deeper and faster, falling into a perfect rhythm. Their bodies rocked back and forth and she arched into him, holding onto his sides. The tension strained through their muscles, fighting for the release they longed for.

As he pushed into her, she arched her back and slammed down onto him. Faster and deeper, they met each other's thrusts. They climbed the mountain, both seeking the apex. Their moans mixed with grunts, until she screamed his name and he had a fleeting thought to be thankful they were out in the woods were no one would hear them.

"Oh, Trever!" She arched her body against his, and her core muscles tightened against his shaft as her release coursed through her. Her nails dug into his chest, no doubt leaving deep welts and angry red scratches behind, but he didn't care.

He continued to pump into her, never missing a beat. The tightening of her around his shaft was all he needed to find his own apex. He arched his hips, sending him deep within her, and let himself go over the edge.

"Fuck, Allie," he growled, pulling her down against his chest.

"I think that's what we just did," she joked, her eyes closed and her fingers teasing over his stomach. "Though we might have to do it again, just to be sure."

"You're trying to kill me, aren't you?" His shaft twitched at her words. He wanted her again and as many times as he could before she realized she made a mistake by letting him back into her heart.

"Not yet." She slipped off him and collapsed onto the bed next to him. "I think you need sleep before we can do anything again."

He tugged a blanket up from the bottom of the bed and covered them both. She snuggled against him and his fingers caressed along her side in lazy strokes. He wanted to keep her right there, in his arms, where he knew she was safe.

"I love you, Allie."

"I love you too." She ran her hand up his chest and stopped below his bullet wound. "I'm sorry you got shot, but thank you for coming to my aid."

"I'd go to the ends of the world for you." He hugged her tighter against him. "My forever…"

Chapter Nine

Sidelined

Morning arrived all too early, making Allyson want to groan. When she opened her eyes and found Trever smiling down at her the grumpiness disappeared. She had woken numerous times in the night just to look up at him and make sure she hadn't dreamed the whole thing. He was really back. Not even in her life twenty-four hours and she had already fallen into bed naked with him.

It didn't seem too fast considering she'd known him all of her life. What concerned her was the fact she wasn't even worried he would leave again. She wasn't sure if she believed he was there to stay or if she knew she'd survive if he decided to leave. She was determined to enjoy every moment she had with him. *Live every moment to its fullest.*

"Good morning." He rolled toward her, kissing along the curve of her neck.

"Later. I need a shower and we have work to do."

"What work? I thought we gave that up so we could spend the rest of our lives in bed allowing me to cherish every inch of your body."

"You wish." She arched back from him. "Vezio Persichetti, does that ring any bells? Or does the name only strike fear into my heart?"

Trever stopped kissing her neck and moved back. "After today you won't have to worry about him or anyone with ties to him. I'm going to take care of that problem."

"I hope so. It's only been a few days since this started and I already feel like I've aged a dozen years." She dragged her fingers through her hair, pushing the mass of curls out of her face. "I can't go on like this."

"Don't worry." He pressed his lips to her forehead. "It will all be over later today and we'll be on our way to Chicago. Anthony's body will be released to you once this is settled and I'll make arrangements for him to be transported to Montana as well. There's nothing here for you any longer but there's a lot in Montana. You'll be surrounded by people who care about you. You haven't met Ethan's fiancé yet, have you?"

"I've spoken with Donna but no I haven't met her yet." Ethan used to come spend two weeks every summer at the ranch when they were kids and they had always been close. Even though it had been awhile since she'd seen him she knew it would be like not a day had gone by when she did. They had a friendship where it didn't matter how long it had been since they were together, it picked up where it left off. They'd be laughing and joking before she even unpacked. He was someone anyone could call on at any time and he'd be there. He'd proven it by sending Trever to her aid.

"It will be good to see him again and meet Donna."

"And thank him for sending me?" He raised an eyebrow at her.

"I don't think so." She pushed against his chest lightly. "Even though it worked out, he's still in trouble for that. It could have been disastrous and then what? We'd have been stuck together ready to kill each other. Or you could have got here and refused to come into the motel when he told you I was the one in need."

"Not a chance. I'd have rushed into a burning building for you. I think I've proven that by taking a bullet for you." He jumped off the bed, putting distance between them.

She took hold of one of the pillows and flung it at him. "I'll give you another bullet hole if you don't watch it." Even as she said it she was laughing. "I guess you've proven yourself worthy."

"You guess?" He strolled around the bed and she couldn't take her gaze off his naked body. "I'll be sure to prove it again before we leave. First I've got to make a phone call to the jail administrator to make arrangements for my visit with Vezio."

"I'm coming with you." She pulled herself upright and leaned back against the pillows.

"The fuck you are." He grabbed his jeans from the floor near the doorway where they had been left the night before. "There's no doubt his men are hanging around the area and you will not be anywhere near it. I prefer you stay here. No one followed us and you'll be safe here. If you press me, I'll drop you off with a friend of mine who can keep an eye on you." He tugged the jeans up over his hips. "Or my favorite option is handcuffing you to the bed while I'm gone. Though I don't think you'd like that much considering I could be gone for a couple hours. It's a forty-minute drive each way. So, consider that before you open your mouth and push the issue."

"Trever, this is insane. Someone could show up here and I'd be all alone."

"You're safer here than going there and you know it. Vezio's reach is too far, someone could have seen us driving through town and call one of his guys." He paused to tug his shirt over his head. "Your father taught you how to shoot when you were young, have you kept up with it?"

"Yeah, but I don't have a gun with me. I have my concealed weapons permit, another thing Dad made me get when I was of age, though I rarely carry."

"That's fine. I'll leave you one. I don't expect you'll need it. You'll stay inside with the doors locked until I return and you'll be fine."

There was no debate in his tone. Even though he had given her options, he had already made up his mind. He was leaving her here while he went off and dealt with Vezio. She didn't like it but he did have a point someone might see her and before Trever could end this mess she'd end up dead. This disaster that she found herself in kept tearing at her. She didn't like being kept on the sidelines and protected, but she'd called for help, and now she had to sit back and accept it.

Chapter Ten
Skirting the Line

Trever called in every favor he had and nearly every old buddy just to get five minutes alone with Vezio Persichetti and not have a second of it recorded. He was working on the outskirts of the law to protect Allie. He wasn't planning on going into details with Ethan about how far he'd skirted the line. At the end of all of this, the only thing that mattered was Allie's safety.

He stood in the middle of one of the lawyer visiting rooms waiting. He wasn't a lawyer, but this was one place he could be assured there would be no cameras and no one listening in on their conversation. It also put the administrator at ease because he didn't have to explain things to his staff. He'd let everyone assume Trever was part of Vezio's legal staff and he'd be gone before anyone questioned things.

Leaving Allie alone at the cottage weighed on him like a ton of cement and he fought the urge to pace the constricting space. Though he'd been in spaces so tight he had to wiggle his way out, this jailhouse room was closing in on him. He wiped his damp hands on the legs of his jeans. The minute the door opened all of his unease disappeared and he shot into action.

Vezio entered looking smug. His dark black hair was slicked back and the orange jumpsuit made him appear wider than he was. For someone running the drug trade in the area, who'd gotten his nickname—Steel—from beating people with a steel crowbar, he didn't appear to have too much muscle. The men under him must have been the ones who dished out the dirty work, leaving Vezio to stand back and watch the show. Now that he had his nickname and people feared him, he didn't have to work as hard, and that showed.

Vezio took a seat at the metal table bolted to the floor and the guard at the door nodded to Trever before closing it. Gangster versus SEAL, round one was about to begin.

"Who are you?" The Brooklyn accent made Trever pause for a moment.

"The name's Trever…Trever Alexander. I grew up not far from here but it's been years since I've been home."

"You working with my lawyer?"

"No." He stepped up next to the table so Vezio had to look up at him. "I'm here to offer you a deal of sorts."

"If you're with the D.A.'s office you'll have to discuss any deals with my attorneys." Vezio started to rise.

"I think you'd better stay seated and hear me out." Trever waited a moment while Vezio decided if he wanted to listen or not. When the other man lowered himself back onto the chair he continued. "Seems we had a mutual friend—Anthony Mason."

"That grifter owe you money too? Well I hate to be the one to inform you, he's gone to his grave owing it to you." Laughing, Vezio leaned back again in the chair.

"I know. You killed him."

The laughter died and Vezio sat up straight. "Says who?"

"The survivor." As much as Trever was enjoying this he needed to get down to it before his time was up.

"You a cop?"

"No." He paused for a moment letting that sink in. "Like I said, I'm here to offer you a deal. You call your men off her and she'll keep her mouth shut about what she saw. You've got enough charges already, you don't need a murder one on top of it."

"There are other ways to make that problem disappear."

"That's where you're wrong. You or your men come after her again and I'll be the least of your problems. You'll never make it out of prison alive, and whoever you assign to do the deed won't get within a hundred yards." Trever leaned forward, placing his palms on the table. "Call off your men and see the sun rise tomorrow. Fuck with me and you'll be looking up from the fiery pits of Hell."

"Who's she to you? Seems mighty important to you."

"She's innocent. In the wrong place at the wrong time. Anthony dragged her down with him. She doesn't deserve to pay for his sins." He reached down to the chair in front of him and pulled up a paper sack. "Word is Anthony owed you two grand. You agree to leave her be and this is yours. Five grand. I've made arrangements with the staff here and it will be given to the guy of your choice, no questions asked. The decision is yours."

"What insurance do I have she hasn't already gone to the police with her claims?"

"My word." Trever shrugged. What did this guy want? "You'll know for sure when no murder charges are added to your list of crimes. Think of it this way: if I'm lying you won't just be able to send your men after her but me as well. You'll get two for the price of one, plus five grand."

"You're risking a lot for this whore, including your life."

Trever slammed his hand down onto the table. "Don't call her that."

"Just like I thought, she's not someone you're protecting, you're hooked on her. Your doll could get herself killed if you don't keep a better eye on her."

"Is that a threat?" Trever snatched the paper bag off the table. "Should I assume you don't want this deal? Think carefully before you answer because murder charges with her testifying and even your high powered attorneys won't be able to get you off."

"You really think she'd live to testify?" Vezio let out a deep laugh. "You're stupider than you look."

"I know she'll be alive, because she'll have a group of Navy SEALs protecting her and there's not a chance you'll get through us. How many of us are you willing to take on to get to a woman who only wants to put all of this behind her? Don't start something you can't finish, because I've never backed down from a fight and I'll promise you one thing. If you come after her again it will be you who won't live to see the inside of the courtroom." Done, Trever stepped toward the door.

"She's Anthony's sister, isn't she?"

Trever's silence was all Vezio needed to confirm his suspicions.

"Fine."

"What was that?"

"I'll get word to my men. Anthony was good for some things, better before he got hooked, and worked for me for years. I'll respect his memory and let her live as long as she doesn't cause problems for me. You, on the other hand, watch your back. If I see you in these parts again fair is fair."

"Don't worry, we're leaving this town and putting everything behind us." Trever held up the bag. "This will be with the administrator. Your guys have seventy-two hours to collect it."

"I'll get it myself. I suspect my attorneys will have me out on bond before the day is over."

"Guard." Trever knocked on the door, letting them know he was done. "Good doing business with you."

"Yeah. Keep your doll under wraps. I don't want to see her end up in trouble," Vezio called after him as he strolled out of the room.

"She's got the best protection," Trever mumbled more to himself than

Vezio as the door shut and he was face to face with Ben, the jail's administrator. With a nod he held out the bag. "Thanks, man. I owe you one."

"Damn right you do." Ben took the sack and turned to lead him out. "Now get back to her. Get out of town before he's had time to reconsider and send some of his goons after you."

"I've got to stop by her apartment to get some of her things and then we're gone." Trever stood near the door leading him back to fresh air and freedom. "Don't worry, I don't think he's a threat any longer, at least not for us. For this town, that's a different story. Do you think there's a strong enough case against him?"

"Not a chance." Ben shook his head grimly. "He's got a strong legal team and they've already gone to work on half of the evidence that was gathered and had it dismissed. We'll be lucky if he spends the night in jail, let alone a conviction on his pending charges."

Strolling out of the jail, Trever noticed a weight lifted off his shoulders. Vezio would be an issue if their paths crossed again, but for now they were able to squeak by with only a few scrapes. However, everything he had said in there was true. Even if something happened to him, he knew that Ethan, Lucas, and those SEALs he served with would keep Allie safe. She was part of a family closer than she realized. She was his and that meant something more than the ring he planned to give her or the piece of paper that would declare them husband and wife. She was his other half, his better half, and she held his heart.

Chapter Eleven:
Welcome to Montana

Two days later, Allyson stepped off the plane in Montana with Trever by her side. The sky was painted with pinks, yellows, and blues as the sun sank into the horizon. It seemed fitting to the new life she was beginning here. Patrick strolled down the plane steps, his suit jacket unbuttoned, and a smile spreading across his face. After they stopped in Chicago, Patrick had insisted on flying with them back to Montana instead of them waiting for a commercial flight. It had given Allyson time to catch up on all the changes in Patrick's life, though it had also denied her the opportunity to spend some private time with Trever. Something was different about him since his visit to the jail and she couldn't put her finger on it. He said everything went fine, that Vezio wouldn't be a problem for them again. If that was true, what was on his mind?

"I'm afraid this is where we go our separate ways." Patrick held out a hand to her.

She ignored the hand and wrapped her arms around him. "It was great seeing you again and thank you for everything."

"Even for giving that pipsqueak the keys to my jet to come find you?" Patrick joked and glanced back at his brother. "I'm not sure I believe this whole story about the gangster after innocent Allyson Mason. I think he was trying to con me into letting him use the plane as a way to seduce you."

"I assure you that I didn't even know about the plane until after…" Her cheeks burned with embarrassment. "Umm…"

"On that note I'm going to get her out of here." Trever slipped his arm around her waist. "I believe she's sleep deprived."

"Yeah, that must be it." She bit her lip. "Sorry, Patrick, I umm…"

"You're beautiful when you're embarrassed." He laughed. "I'm glad you two reconnected and I expect an invite to the wedding."

"Get out of here before I steal your plane again." Trever's voice was tight as he eyed his brother.

Was it her imagination or did Trever tense at the mention of a wedding? She tried not to read too much into it. Trever whisked her away, heading toward the parking lot, a porter directly behind them with their bags.

"What's wrong?" she asked him.

"You wanted to stop by Ethan's and visit with him so we've got to hurry." He tipped his head to the porter and slipped some money from his pocket. "Just throw the bags in the bed."

Stifling a yawn, she paused next to the truck as he opened the passenger door. "It's been a long day and I think we need to talk. Can we just go to your place?"

"It's not as nice as whatever accommodations Ethan has for you at his place."

"I don't care as long as you're there." She stepped closer to him and placed her hand on his chest. "I want to curl up in your arms and sleep. I know I'll be safe and right now I really need that. But if you don't want me there then take me to Ethan's. Maybe we can get together tomorrow or something…" Those words tightened her throat. Was she losing him again?

"Get in."

Unsure where they were going she did as he asked. He was her ride and

Ethan had already done enough she wasn't going to call him to the airport to pick her up because Trever wouldn't take her back to his place. He walked around the front of the truck and a moment later he climbed in next to her, started the engine, and pulled out of the parking garage without a word.

Every second of his silence rubbed another layer off her nerves. Looking out the window, she felt like she was watching as her world crumbled under her fingers and she wasn't sure what to do to make it better. Now that Vezio wasn't a threat, was that it? Would Trever leave again? What happened to everything he said at the cottage?

"Maybe it's best you take me to Ethan's."

"The fuck I will." He sped through the streets until the buildings rushed by her in a blur. "You said you wanted to come home with me and you will."

"You don't want me there…" He hadn't said it but the silence spoke volumes. Or was she reading too much into it?

"Bullshit." His grip tightened on the wheel until his knuckles turned white. "I want you with me, always."

"What changed?" She pressed her back against the door to look at him. "What happened with Vezio? If he isn't an issue then what is? Because something is different."

"Vezio won't cause you any problems as long as your paths don't cross again."

He made a sharp turn, fishtailing the truck enough that she grabbed hold of the dash. "Damn it, Trever, slow down before you kill us."

"We're almost there."

"We're not going to make it if you get us into an accident." Her stomach roiled as he skidded to a halt, turning into a parking garage. "Where the hell are we going?"

"My place." A moment later they were parked on the second floor of the garage and he turned to her. "You wanted to be here."

"Do you want me here?" The distance between them made her need to hear him say the words. She needed to know this wasn't a mistake. That everything that happened in Texas wasn't just because they had been caught up in the moment. "Trever—"

"Fuck it." He slid across the front seat until he had her pinned between him and the door. "I love you, Allie. I knew that before I left to deal with Vezio, but when I left him I realized something."

"What's that?"

A woman strolled past them, eyeing them suspiciously as she climbed into a car further down the lane.

"I don't want to go back to the way things were. I want you in my life. Today, tomorrow, next year, and a dozen years from now. I want you as my wife. Marry me, Allie."

"What?" Her jaw slacked and her mouth fell open.

"Marry me. We've been apart for years and I don't want to spend another day away from you. I want you in my life in a permanent way." He took her hands into his, interlocking their fingers. "There's never been anyone else for either of us. Not seriously anyways, and not anyone we've loved like we love each other."

"It's been forty-eight hours since you found me again and you...you're proposing?"

"Can you actually sit there and tell me that you don't want this? That you're not still in love with me like you were before?" He paused waiting for her to answer and when she didn't say anything he nodded. "I thought so."

"We're different people than we were then." Even as she tried to explain why this was insane she wanted to say yes. It's what she wanted years ago and what she had always hoped would happen. Someday he'd leave the military behind and would come back to Texas, back to her.

"We're smarter and we know what we want. I stood there knowing you were in danger and I knew I couldn't let you go again. I want you in my life forever. The marriage license is a piece of paper, but I want us to have it. I want to shout my love for you from the rooftops, to do it in front of our friends and family. Most importantly, I want you. You're my other half and you hold my heart. Say yes, I know you want to."

"This is crazy." She let out a light, nervous chuckle.

His hands cupped the sides of her face. "The best decisions in life are crazy. Allyson Marie Mason, I once told you I couldn't promise you the forever that you deserved, but I was wrong. I can't imagine life without you by my side. You are my forever and the woman I love. Will you marry me?"

"Yes." A tear rolled down her cheek and she nodded.

Screw crazy. If all of this taught me anything it's that life is too short. Grab your forever with both hands and hold on.

He pressed his lips against hers, claiming her and steaming up the windows.

A knock on the window had a shriek ripping from her lips. Trever pulled back, his hand going under his seat, pulling a gun from underneath and he pressed his finger to his lips warning her to be quiet.

"Are you guys getting out of the truck tonight?"

"Fuck, Ethan, are you trying to get yourself killed?" Trever reached over and hit the button for the window. "What the hell are you doing here?"

"After I spoke with you earlier I figured you wouldn't be coming over tonight. I wanted to make sure Allyson was okay." He placed his arm on the window frame. "Hi, cuz. He treating you okay?"

"You asshole." Trever grabbed an empty soda bottle from the cup holder and threw it at Ethan. "You're interrupting something."

"You mean a marriage proposal?" The corner of Ethan's mouth curled up into a half smile and he glanced at Allyson. "So what did you say?"

"You knew?" She glanced at Trever and then back at Ethan.

"He didn't tell me. I overheard it all while I was waiting for you to get out of the truck." Ethan grabbed the door handle, pulled open the door, and gestured to the bags sitting on the ground. "You didn't even hear me grab the suitcases from the bed of the truck."

"You make it sound like that's a big accomplishment. Marines are *known* for sneaking up on people." Trever pulled the keys from the ignition and tucked them into his pocket.

"It is when I'm sneaking up on a Navy SEAL. You should have been more on guard. What if Vezio's men followed you?"

"We've come to an understanding." Trever stepped out of the truck. "Since you've decided to drop by unannounced, why don't we continue this conversation upstairs?"

"I'm waiting to find out Allyson's answer. Are there congratulations in order or not? 'Cause if not maybe I should load her bag into my—"

"I think there's something in the water here in Montana." She glanced at Ethan, before looking over at Trever, and then back to Ethan. "You're both cocky, nosy, and full of yourselves."

"Well two out of three comes from us being the best," Ethan joked.

"The two of you are too much." She shook her head and started to get out of the truck. "To answer your question, I said yes. But if you say another word, I won't invite you to the wedding."

"I'll risk it." When she stepped out of the truck he wrapped his arms around her, bringing her in for a hug. "I'm glad you're okay and I'm sorry about Anthony."

"Thanks…" Her voice broke and she held onto him for a moment. It was good to see him. The time apart had been too long. She had planned to make it back for their engagement party, kind of as a surprise but also because she was dying to meet Donna. Instead she'd spent that weekend in the hospital with Anthony after he overdosed *again*. "I look forward to meeting Donna in person.

We've chatted often enough on the phone I feel like I've already known her for years."

"Tomorrow you guys can come over for lunch before Trever's appointment."

"What appointment?" She glanced back at Trever only to find him shrugging.

"The doctor we spoke about on the phone, he had a cancelation, so I've booked it for you. It's best to get in right away and take care of these migraines." Ethan stepped back and grabbed one of the suitcases.

"You just want me up to par so you can start dishing out assignments to me. The less you have to worry about the more time you can spend with your fiancé." Trever grabbed the other bag and slipped his arm around Allyson's waist. "Ready, sweetie?"

She wasn't sure, but still she nodded. Walking into Trever's apartment was the first step into her new life. She'd left everything behind in Texas and was starting over. He was by her side and that's what she had wanted since they were eighteen. However, starting over again in a new city was frightening. At least she knew a few people there and she wouldn't be completely alone. A new start on life should be exciting. It meant she could do anything she wanted, so why was she nervous? Maybe it was all she had lost along the way and the people that weren't there to share this new adventure with her. Her heart ached that her father and Anthony weren't by her side.

You'll always be in my heart…

Epilogue

Ten months before, Allyson had been apprehensive about her new life in Montana, even with Trever by her side. Now here she stood in front of the white two-story colonial farmhouse with the honey brown shutters and large porch, rubbing the small bump of her stomach. Everything had worked out better than she could have expected.

They had waited six months to walk down the aisle, giving her time to adjust, and Trever had wanted his post-concussion syndrome to be better controlled on the migraine medication. He said he didn't want her to be stuck with a defective husband. To her it wouldn't have mattered if the migraines continued, she'd have still married him.

Everything was working out and the migraines had disappeared. Vezio's attorneys got most of the pending charges against him dropped and the couple that stuck he was found innocent of. Money had paid off those that could be and the others were afraid of what would happen if Vezio was convicted. Even if she had tried to bring murder charges against him, he'd have most likely found a way to get around them. In the end it looked like that had turned out okay. At least he hadn't caused any problems for them and they were able to put that all behind them.

"What do you think, Mrs. Alexander? Is it everything you hoped it would be?" Trever came up behind her and wrapped his arms around her, laying his hands over hers.

"It's beautiful." It was more than beautiful. It was more than she could have hoped for when he told her what Patrick had come to Montana to meet with him about. While the house was a close match to the one she grew up in back in Texas, the land surrounding it was larger, with more cattle, horses, and a lot more work than she had expected. "Are you sure about this?"

"I am." His hand slid down to her stomach. "I want our child to know the joys of what we had. To be raised on a ranch with more animals than they know what to do with. Where they can run free and we don't have to worry about them running into the street and getting hit by a car, or kidnapped from our front yard. We were raised to be independent, to respect our elders, and to be hardworking. There wasn't another way when you lived on a ranch. Don't you remember the joys of it when we were kids?"

She nodded. "I never thought I'd leave the ranch. It was more than just where I grew up, it was home. There was no freer time than to be out on horseback rounding up the cattle with Dad. Galloping through the acres with the wind in your hair."

"There was always somewhere we could sneak off to when we wanted to be alone." He pressed his lips to her neck just below her ear. "Think of all the memories we can make here, all we can give our children."

"A ranch…" Looking back on everything they'd been through, she'd have never figured they'd end up there. Being forced to sell the family ranch and then leaving Texas for good she thought her ranching days were over. Now, five months pregnant, she found herself staring out onto their land. It was a fifteen-minute drive to downtown, close enough that they'd be able to continue the life they started there. It was perfect because Donna and she had grown close over the last few months. They were the first girlfriends she had since high school.

"I never thought we'd end up here but what can I say? When the owner wanted to retire Patrick bought him out. This place is one of the best providers for Alexander Distribution and he didn't want to lose it. The house is remodeled and the staff keeps the ranch running smoothly, but he needs someone to oversee the place. That's where we come in. We can still turn him down."

"No!" The word was out of her mouth before she thought she even knew the answer. "I guess I want to stay. I think our little girl agrees." She took hold of his wrist, moving his hand over to where she'd felt the baby kick for the first time.

"Is that...?" Without moving his hand, he came around to stand in front of her. "Our son is kicking."

She tipped her head back and laughed. "Our daughter," she stated again, a little firmer.

"Boy or girl, it doesn't matter as long as our child is healthy." His grin spread across his face. "The best thing is, by overseeing this ranch I'm not going to miss a moment of this baby's life. No missions, assignments, or anything that will take me away from the two of you."

"I wonder if we can put up with having you around that much." She laid her hand on his chest. "It will sure be different having you around again. Ethan has been keeping you pretty busy with Safety First Security assignments since we got back from our honeymoon."

"How about we go inside and make up for lost time?" He took her hand in his. "I love you, Allie."

"I love you too. Today, tomorrow, and forever."

Marissa Dobson

Marissa Dobson is a USA Today Bestselling Author of more than sixty books in different genres of romance, including Alaskan Tigers series.

Being the first daughter to an avid reader gave her the advantage of learning to read at a young age. Since then she has always had her nose in a book. It wasn't until she was a teenager that she started exploring writing.

Marissa lives an hour from Washington D.C. with her supportive husband, Thomas—who puts up with all her quirks and listens to her brainstorm in the middle of the night—and her writing buddy Pup Cameron, a cocker spaniel.

Also by Marissa Dobson

Alaskan Tigers:

Tiger Time

The Tiger's Heart

Tigress for Two

Night with a Tiger

Trusting a Tiger

Alaskan Tigers Box Set Vol. 1

Jinx's Mate

Two for Protection

Bearing Secrets

Tiger Tracks

Healing the Clan

Alaskan Tigers Box Set Vol. 2

Her Black Tiger

Tiger Trouble

Alpha Claimed

Roaring to be Claimed

Forever Creek Shifters:

Forever's Fight

Protecting Forever

Crimson Hollow:

Romancing the Fox

Loving the Bears

A Lion's Chance

Swift Move

Purrable Lion

Bearly Alive

Saved by a Lion

Furever Mated Box Set

SEALed for You:

Ace in the Hole

Explosive Passion

Operation Family

Marine for You:

Lucky Chance

Back from Hell

A Marine's Second Chance

Phantom Security:

Different Sides

Undercover Agent

Takeover Agent

Cedar Grove Medical:

Hope's Toy Chest

Destiny's Wish

Leena's Dream

Cedar Grove Medical Box Set

Fate:

Snowy Fate

Sarah's Fate

Mason's Fate

As Fate Would Have It

Half Moon Harbor Resort:

Learning to Live

Learning What Love Is

Her Cowboy's Heart

Half Moon Harbor Resort Vol. 1

Tanner Cycles:

Until Sydney

Stormkin:

Storm Queen

Blessing Montana:

Smoke

Touch of Home

United Homefront Ranch:

Destination Heaven

Beyond Monogamy:

Theirs to Treasure

Reaper:

Touch of Death

Clearwater:

Winterbloom

Unexpected Forever

Losing to Win

Christmas Countdown

The Surrogate

Clearwater Romance Volume One

Small Town Doctor

Stand Alone:

SEALed Rescue

Past Comes to Light

SEALed Outcome

Starting Over

Secret Valentine

Restoring Love